Pinkalicious®
Crazy Hair Day

HARPER FESTIVAL
An Imprint of HarperCollinsPublishers

by Victoria Kann

To Ian, who has a crazy hair day almost every day!

The author gratefully acknowledges the
artistic and editorial contributions of
Dynamo, Kirsten Berger, and Amanda Glickman.

HarperFestival is an imprint of HarperCollins Publishers.

Pinkalicious: Crazy Hair Day
Copyright © 2014 by Victoria Kann

PINKALICIOUS and all related logos and characters are trademarks of Victoria Kann
Used with permission.

Based on the HarperCollins book *Pinkalicious*
written by Victoria Kann and Elizabeth Kann, illustrated by Victoria Kann
All rights reserved. Printed in the United States of America.
No part of this book may be used or reproduced in any manner whatsoever without
written permission except in the case of brief quotations embodied in critical articles and reviews.
For information address HarperCollins Children's Books,
a division of HarperCollins Publishers, 195 Broadway, New York, NY 10007.
www.harpercollinschildrens.com

Library of Congress catalog card number: 2013944035
ISBN 978-0-06-218768-0

Book design by Kirsten Berger
17 18 CWM 10 9
❖
First Edition

Piiiiink . . . piiiiink . . . piiiiink rang my alarm clock.
My pink bows went flying! I was already up.
I'd been trying different hair styles all morning.

"Mommy! Mommy!" I called.
"It's Crazy Hair Day at school!"
My hair would be the craziest.
I didn't see Mommy in the kitchen.
I opened the fridge.
"Get ready, hair, to be pinkafied!"
Mommy once said lemon juice helps turn
hair blond, so I bet cranberry juice would help
my hair turn . . . PINK!

CRANBERRY

I poured a big glass of juice and leaned down to dip my hair in it.

"Pinkalicious!" Mommy yelled.

I froze.

The ends of my hair touched the juice.

"Juice is for drinking. You may not put it in your hair."

"But I want to have pink hair!" I said.

"I have another idea," Mommy said, "so you won't be a bee magnet."

Bees! Ahh!

I hadn't thought of that.

Mommy bent two big pipe cleaners and braided a pigtail around each one.

My hair looked like it was floating!

"My braids are antigravity!"
As I leaped to the bus stop, I pretended I was an astronaut.
I couldn't wait to show Rose.

Finally, the bus came.
"I'm an astronaut in search of Planet Pink!"

I bounced in my space shoes, searching the galaxy for Rose.
There she was!
Uh-oh.

I felt like I was looking into a mirror.
"Oh, look! You guys are copycats!"
Tiffany said.
Everyone laughed at us.
I sat down next to my friend.
"Who cares what Tiffany thinks?" I said.
Rose smiled, but not a big smile.
My braids felt droopy.

At school, we all crowded into our classroom.
Brittany had hair like a volcano!
Sophia's hairdo was like a beehive.
Molly sat next to me and Rose.
Her hair was fluffed up like a puffy cloud.

History of Hair

Mr. Pushkin had put up a huge poster.
It said, HISTORY OF HAIR.
It was hair-sterical.
There were so many funny styles.

Mr. Pushkin told us all about history through hairdos.

When I looked at Tiffany's hair, I saw that it looked like a 1960s hippie hairdo.

Alex had taped muttonchop sideburns onto his face. They were from the 1800s.

Then I saw it.

Right in the middle of the poster was a beautiful hairstyle worn by a queen.

I had an idea!

At recess, I yelled to Rose, "Follow me!" We ran to the edge of the field. There were pink and purple flowers everywhere.

Rose helped me take out my pipe cleaners and wind them into one big coil.

We piled my hair all around it.

We picked flowers, and Rose stuck them all over my hair.

She even let me borrow her necklace as a finishing touch.

"Do you want a new hairdo, too?" I asked Rose.
"I like my wacky hairstyle the way it is!" Rose said.
"You look fantastic—just like a real queen!"

By the time we were done, it was time to go back inside.

The whole class stared at us!

"I want to wear a necklace in my hair, too," Kendra said.

"I wish I'd thought of using flowers," said Molly.

In front of the whole class, Mr. Pushkin said, "Great work, Rose and Pinkalicious! You two have made hair-story come alive."

It was time for the hair parade!
We marched around the school.
I stood tall like a queen and waved to my royal subjects.

The next morning when I got on the bus, I couldn't believe my eyes.

All the girls had decorations in their hair.

Rose had saved me a seat.

"Who are the copycats now?" she said.

"Maybe every day can be Crazy Hair Day!" I said. "Then no one would ever have a bad hair day!"